To ....

For being good.

MERRY CHRISTMAS!

From Santa

Santa is coming to New Brunswick

Written by Steve Smallman
Illustrated by Robert Dunn
Designed by Sarah Allen

Copyright © Hometown World Ltd. 2014

Published by Sourcebooks Jabberwocky, an imprint of Sourcebooks, Inc.
P.O. Box 4410, Naperville, Illinois 60567-4410
(630) 961-3900
Fax: (630) 961-2168
www.jabberwockykids.com

Library of Congress Cataloging-in-Publication data is on file with the publisher.

Source of Production: Leo Paper Products, Guangdong Province, China
Date of Production: April 2014
Run Number: HTW_PO170314
Printed and bound in China
LEO 10 9 8 7 6 5 4 3 2 1

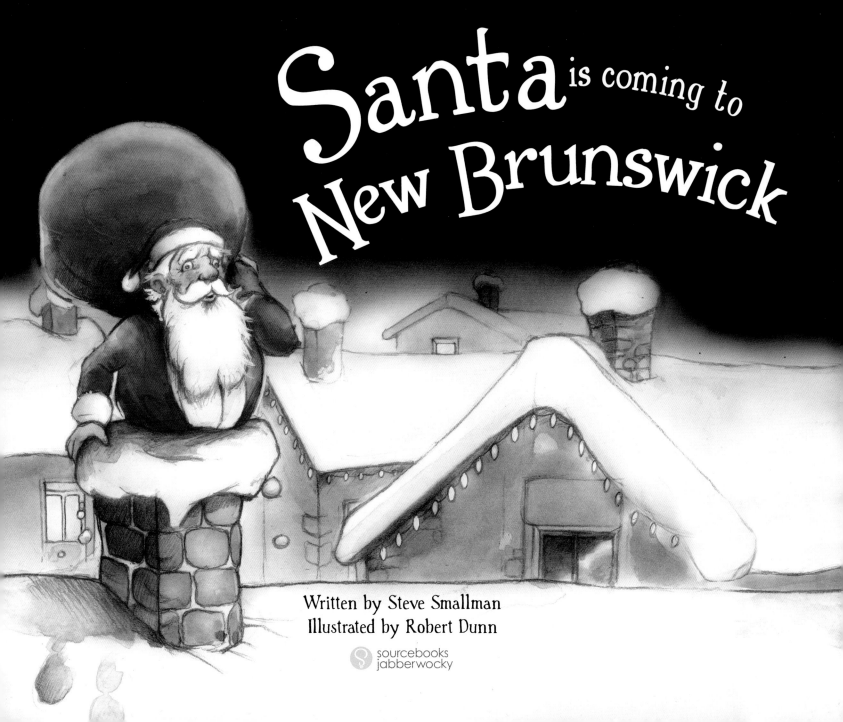

Santa is coming to New Brunswick

Written by Steve Smallman

Illustrated by Robert Dunn

sourcebooks
jabberwocky

"Well?"

boomed Santa. "Have all the children from **New Brunswick** been good this year?"

"Well...uh...mostly," answered the little old elf, as he bustled across the busy workshop to Santa's desk.

Santa peered down at the elf from behind the tall, teetering piles of letters that the children of New Brunswick had sent him.

"Mostly?" asked Santa, looking over the top of his glasses.

"Yes...but they've all been **especially** good in the last few days!" said the elf.

"Jolly good!" chuckled Santa,
"Then we'd better get their presents loaded up!"

Even though the sack of presents was

really, really big

and the elves were **really, really** small,

they seemed to have no trouble loading it onto Santa's sleigh.
Though how they managed to fit such a big sack into one little sleigh
even they didn't know. But somehow they did.

"Splendid!" boomed Santa. "We're ready to go!"

"Er...not quite, Santa," said the little old elf. "One of our reindeer is missing!"

"Missing?

Which reindeer is missing?" asked Santa.

"The youngest one, Santa," said the elf. "It's his first flight tonight. I've called him and called him, but..."

Just then, a young reindeer strolled up, munching on a large carrot.

"Where have you been?"

asked Santa.

But the youngest reindeer was crunching so loudly that it was no wonder he hadn't heard the little old elf calling.

"Oh well, never mind," said Santa, giving the reindeer a little wink.
He took out his Santa-nav and tapped in the coordinates for New Brunswick.
"This will guide us to New Brunswick in no time."

Crunch!
Crunch!
Crunch!

With a flick of the reins and a jerk of the harness, off they went, racing through the sky.

"Ho, ho, ho!"
laughed Santa.

"We'll soon have all these presents
delivered to the Picture Province!"

Santa's sleigh flew through the starry night, heading south across the Arctic Ocean. On they flew in the crisp, wintry air, crossing over Nunavut. In the wink of an eye, the sleigh was flying above Hudson Bay and on toward Quebec. The youngest reindeer was very excited. He had never been away from the North Pole before.

They had just crossed the Saint Lawrence River
when, suddenly, they ran into a blizzard.
Snowflakes whirled around the sleigh.

They couldn't see a thing!

The youngest reindeer was getting a bit worried,
but Santa didn't seem concerned.

"In two miles..."

said the Santa-nav in a bossy lady's voice,

"...keep left at the next star."

"But, ma'am," Santa blustered, "I can't see any stars in all this snow!"
Soon they were

hopelessly lost!

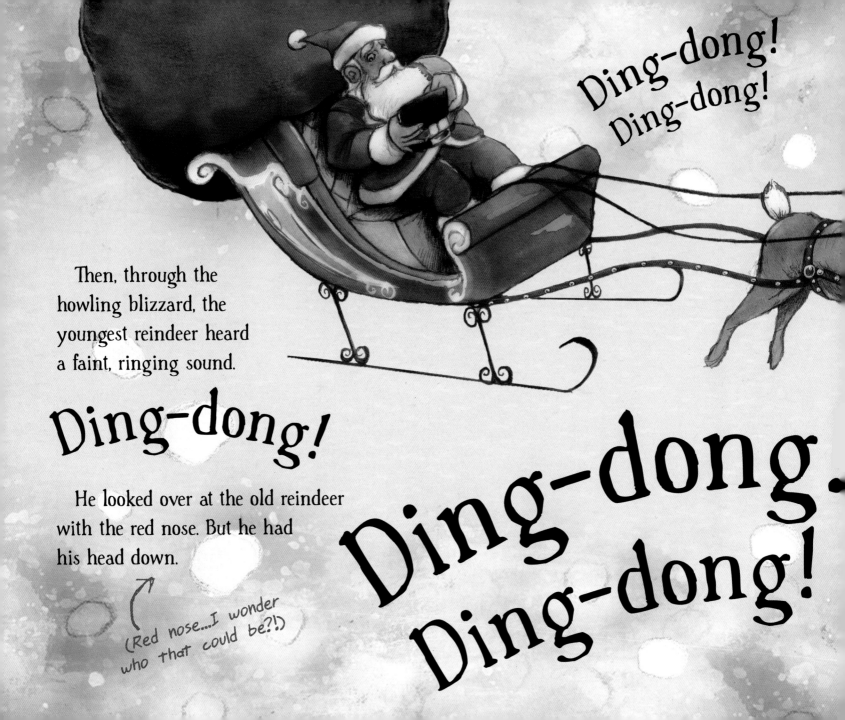

Ding-dong!
Ding-dong!

Then, through the howling blizzard, the youngest reindeer heard a faint, ringing sound.

Ding-dong!

He looked over at the old reindeer with the red nose. But he had his head down.

(Red nose...I wonder who that could be?!)

Ding-dong.
Ding-dong!

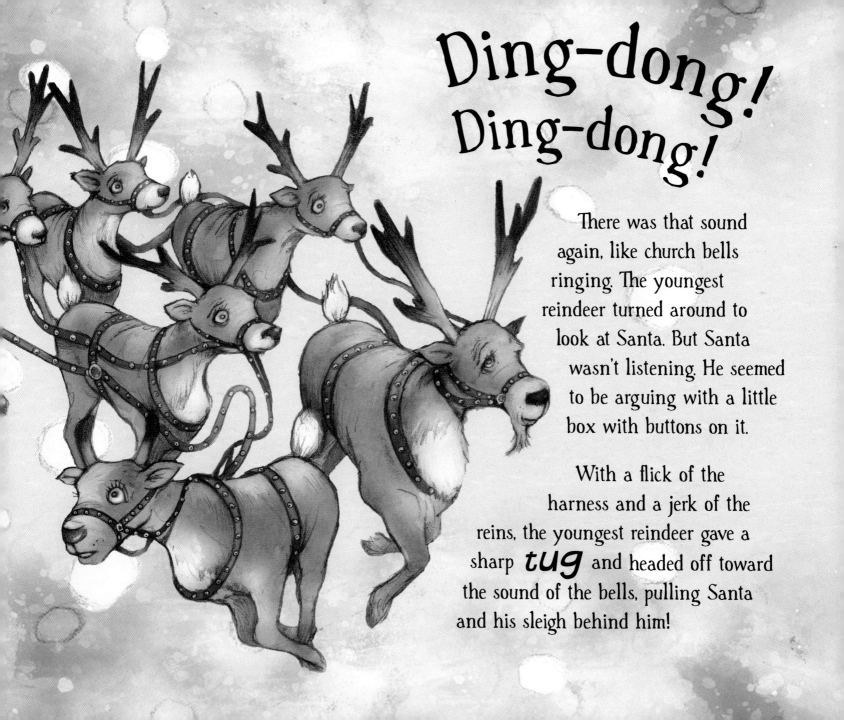

Ding-dong! Ding-dong!

There was that sound again, like church bells ringing. The youngest reindeer turned around to look at Santa. But Santa wasn't listening. He seemed to be arguing with a little box with buttons on it.

With a flick of the harness and a jerk of the reins, the youngest reindeer gave a sharp *tug* and headed off toward the sound of the bells, pulling Santa and his sleigh behind him!

"Whoa!"

cried Santa, pulling his hat straight.
"What's going on?" Then, to his surprise,
he heard the ringing sound.

"Well done, young reindeer!" he shouted cheerfully,
"It must be the bells of the Cathedral of the Immaculate Conception
in Saint John. Don't worry, children, Santa is coming!"

Then, suddenly...

CRUNCH!

The sleigh hit something as it plummeted through the snow clouds. **"You have arrived!"** said the Santa-nav unhelpfully.

Finally, when the snow had died down
and the clouds parted, Santa discovered
exactly where they were...

...stuck, right at the very top of a
Christmas tree near
Market Square!

"Everybody,
PULL!"

The reindeer *pulled* with all their might until, at last, with a screeching noise, the sleigh scraped clear of the Christmas tree. Santa steered them safely over City Hall, past Loyalist House, above Lily Lake, and down into Rockwood Park.

Luckily, there
was no real
damage done, but
the packages had all
been jumbled up. Santa
quickly sorted out the
presents into order again.

"All right," said Santa. "Thanks
to this young reindeer I know where
we are now. Don't worry, children,

Santa is coming!"

Santa drove his sleigh expertly from rooftop to rooftop all over New Brunswick, popping in and out of chimneys as fast as he could go.

(Which was pretty fast for a chubby fellow!)

There were big chimneys in Dieppe and small chimneys in Bathurst. He squeezed down thin chimneys in Bristol and plummeted down fat chimneys in Quispamsis.

The youngest reindeer was
amazed at how quickly they went.
Santa never seemed to get tired at all!
And it looked like all the children in
New Brunswick were going to be very
lucky this year! But the youngest
reindeer was starting to feel
a bit weary and quite
hungry too!

He piled them under the Christmas trees
and carefully filled up the stockings
with surprises.

In house after house, Santa delved
inside his sack for packages of
every shape and size.

Santa took a little bite out of each cookie,
a tiny sip of milk, wiped his beard, and
popped the carrots into his sack.

n house after house, the good children of New
Brunswick had left out a plate of cookies, a
small glass of milk, and a big, crunchy carrot.

From Edmundston to Fredericton, from Campobello Island to Campbellton, from Miramichi to Moncton, from Rothesay to Riverview, and ALL the places in between, Santa and his sleigh visited every house in New Brunswick.

Finally, Santa had delivered the last present on his long New Brunswick list.

"Great moons and stars!" sighed Santa. "It's past midnight and my sack seems as heavy as ever! I hope I haven't forgotten anyone."

Santa opened his sack to check...but it was full of juicy, crunchy carrots!

Santa divided the carrots among all the reindeer.
"Well done!" he said, patting the youngest reindeer gently on the nose.

But the youngest reindeer didn't hear him...he was too busy munching!

Then it was time to set off for home. Santa reset his Santa-nav once more to the North
Pole, and soon they were speeding high above the North Shore, past Mount Carleton, over
the Hopewell Rocks, and out across the Bay of Fundy through the crisp, starry night.